P9-DFB-538

For Starters...

Use these prompts to spark conversation as you read the book aloud.

PAGE 7 – This sounds like it's going to be a real **adventure**—where something exciting happens. What are you **curious** about in the story?

PAGE 8 – Can you guess what this thing is? What clues in the story made you guess that?

PAGE 13 – Why do you think the friends can't figure out what the thing is?

PAGE 14 – Do you think that Owl is really **exhausted**? I wonder why he thinks he needs to make excuses for himself and is getting so irritated.

PAGE 16 – It's no fun when you think you've just been on **a wild goose chase** and all your hard work hasn't paid off. Have you ever felt like that?

PAGE 19 – I can just picture myself going back to get something like that thing. What would make you want to go back for it if you were Squirrel?

PAGE 27 – Well, that thing really **transformed** Squirrel's house! What do you like about this ending to the story?

IN THE WORLD OF BOOKS: We call this kind of story a fantasy because things happen that never could in real life. For instance, the animals act like people.

©2005 Scholastic Inc. All rights reserved.

No part of this publication may be reproduced or stored in a retrieval system,
or transmitted in any form or by any means, electronic, mechanical, photocopying,
recording, or otherwise, without written permission of the publisher.
For information regarding permission, write to: Scholastic Inc.,
Attention: Permissions Department, 557 Broadway, New York, NY 10012.

Published by Scholastic Inc.
90 Old Sherman Turnpike, Danbury, CT 06816

SCHOLASTIC and associated logos are trademarks and/or
registered trademarks of Scholastic Inc.

ISBN 0-7172-8603-7

Printed in the U.S.A.
First Scholastic Printing, November 2005

WORD ADVANTAGE 220

What Did Squirrel Find?

By Susan Hill

Illustrated by Jacqueline East

SCHOLASTIC INC.

New York   Toronto   London   Auckland   Sydney
Mexico City   New Delhi   Hong Kong   Buenos Aires

One warm spring day, Squirrel was searching for the nuts he'd buried last fall. It was quite an **adventure** each year, trying to remember where he'd hidden each one. Squirrel licked his lips at the thought of all those **scrumptious** nuts, and soon he came upon something buried among the roots of a tree.

"What's this?" Squirrel was **curious**. It was clearly not a nut. He **peered** at the strange object, then poked at it. It ticked, and it felt kind of warm when he held it, and it glowed a little.

Squirrel carried the thing to the stream and **plunged** it into the water to wash off the dirt. He was **enthusiastic** and hopeful it would be a tasty treat. Then he licked the shiny shell.

"Yuck! Not something to eat. I'll see if anybody knows what this odd thing is," he said, and **scampered** off to show his friends.

"A very s-s-strange thing, indeed," said Snake, when Squirrel showed her the thing. Snake **slithered** over to take a closer look.

"Yesssss," she agreed. "It's most unusual."

"Well, what do you suppose it is?" Squirrel asked.

"I don't know. You'd better ask Bear," said Snake.

"Hmmmm, where did you get this thing?" asked Bear, suddenly **suspicious**. "Did you steal it?"

"Of course not!" Squirrel **sputtered**. "I dug it up!"

"Sorry for the **misunderstanding**," Bear mumbled.

"I thought it was a walnut!" said Squirrel.

"It's not a walnut, anybody can see it's not a walnut!" said Bear.

"Then what do you suppose it is?" Squirrel **wondered**.

Bear scratched his head. "It's a **complicated** problem," he said. "Better ask Owl."

Squirrel came upon Owl, who was asleep in a tree.

"Owl!" Squirrel said softly.

"Mmmm?" Owl murmured, half asleep. "Is that you, Squirrel? What a **coincidence**; I was just dreaming about squirrels."

"Listen to this and tell me what it is," said Squirrel, and he held the ticking thing up to Owl's ear.

"It's the sound of a woodpecker a mile away," said Owl.

Then Owl opened one eye and looked at the thing. "**Imposter**!" he yelled at it. "It's not a woodpecker at all!"

"Of course not," Squirrel sighed. Nobody seemed to be able to help.

"Well, I don't know what it is," Owl snapped. "All I know is it's broad daylight and I'm **exhausted**. Don't you know I'm a night owl?"

Squirrel sat on a rock under a shady tree.

"I wish I'd never found you," he said to the thing. "All you do is tick, but you don't talk. I've run around all morning trying to find out what you are, but nobody knows! This has been nothing but **a wild goose chase**."

And with that, Squirrel tossed
the thing over his shoulder and
walked away.

"No point in being upset about it," Moose advised
later. "Does it even matter what that thing was?
It wasn't a nut, that's the important thing to
remember. With all your worrying over something
that wasn't even a nut, I'd say you've gone and
made a mountain out of molehill."

"You're right." said Squirrel. And he started off toward home.

But before he'd walked very far, he began to miss having the thing, even if he couldn't eat it and all it did was tick.

He went back and picked it up.

Squirrel carried the
thing to his tree.

He climbed up the tree,
through the door . . .

. . . and into his house.

He made his dinner. He looked at the thing
while he ate. "At least I don't have to feed
you," he said to it.

Squirrel got ready for bed.

He looked at the thing as he brushed his teeth. "At least you don't have teeth to clean," he said.

Squirrel tried to read his book, but kept looking over at the thing.

"I'm too sleepy to read," he said.

Finally, he turned out the light and pulled up the covers.

Squirrel tried to sleep, but the night was cold and his house was **drafty**.

He looked at the thing.

He looked at the door. He got an idea.

He got out of bed, picked up the thing, and placed it carefully in the door hole.

The thing fit perfectly in the door
and blocked the draft quite nicely.

"I don't know what you are," said Squirrel to the thing, "and I may never know. All I know is that you **transformed** my drafty old tree into a warm, cozy home with your **faint** ticking and soft glow."

Squirrel smiled. "I'm glad I found you. I'm glad you weren't a walnut after all."

And then Squirrel fell fast asleep while
the curious thing kept watch.

What does it mean?

A Wild Goose Chase — trying very hard to do something but not getting anywhere. *(Appears on pg. 16.)*

Adventure — something you do that is exciting and/or out of the ordinary. *(Appears on pg. 7.)*

Coincidence — when two things happen at exactly the same time, but weren't planned that way. *(Appears on pg. 14.)*

Complicated — having lots of different parts or ideas, which make something difficult to understand. *(Appears on pg. 13.)*

Curious — being eager to find out about something. *(Appears on pg. 8.)*

Drafty — the feeling of cold air moving through a room or closed-in place. *(Appears on pg. 24.)*

Enthusiastic — being very interested and excited to do something. *(Appears on pg. 9.)*

Exhausted — feeling very tired and worn out. *(Appears on pg. 14.)*

Faint — hard to hear. *(Appears on pg. 27.)*

Imposter — a person who tries to trick others by pretending to be someone else. *(Appears on pg. 14.)*

Made a Mountain Out of a Molehill — made something that isn't important seem important. *(Appears on pg. 18.)*

Misunderstanding — thinking something is one way when it isn't. *(Appears on pg. 12.)*

Peered — looked very carefully at something. *(Appears on pg. 8.)*

Plunged — pushed in suddenly. *(Appears on pg. 9.)*

Scampered — ran or went quickly and lightly. *(Appears on pg. 9.)*

Scrumptious — great-tasting; delicious. *(Appears on pg. 7.)*

Slithered — slid slowly along a surface. *(Appears on pg. 10.)*

Sputtered — made spitting or popping noises. *(Appears on pg. 12.)*

Suspicious — acting in a way that makes others question what you're doing; feeling as if someone is doing something wrong. *(Appears on pg. 12.)*

Transformed — changed one thing into a completely different thing. *(Appears on pg. 27.)*

Wondered — thought about something you want to know more about. *(Appears on pg. 13.)*